Easy Olympic Sports Readers

Cycling

© 2004 by GRIFFIN PUBLISHING GROUP/United States Olympic Committee

Published by Griffin Publishing Group under license from the United States Olympic Committee. The use of the Olympic-related marks and terminology is authorized by the United States Olympic Committee pursuant to Title 36 *U.S. Code*, Section 220506. United States Olympic Committee, One Olympic Plaza, Colorado Springs, CO 80909.

All rights reserved. No portion of this book may be reproduced in any form without written permission of Griffin Publishing Group and Teacher Created Materials.

10 9 8 7 6 5 4 3 2 1

ISBN   1-58000-111-4
TCM   6134

DIR./OPERATIONS . . . . Robin L. Howland
PROJECT MANAGER . . . . Bryan K. Howland
AUTHOR . . . . Debra J. Housel, M.S. Ed.
EDITOR . . . . Eric Migliaccio
DESIGNER . . . . Phil Garcia
PHOTOGRAPHS . . . . Getty Images
COVER PHOTOS . . . . Mike Powell

                              Published in association with
                              and distributed by:
Griffin Publishing Group   **Teacher Created Materials**
18022 Cowan, Suite 202   6421 Industry Way
Irvine, CA 92614   Westminster, CA 92683
www.griffinpublishing.com   www.teachercreated.com

Manufactured in the United States of America

MIKE POWELL

Cycling is an Olympic sport.

Cyclists ride special bikes made for racing.

These bikes are very light.

MIKE POWELL

This helps cyclists go fast.

All cyclists wear helmets to stay safe.

Some races are held on tracks.

MIKE POWELL

The tracks are made just for the race.

MARK DADSWELL

One of the track races is called the match sprint.

Some cyclists ride in road races.

They bike on roads for many miles.

Another event is mountain bike racing.

MIKE POWELL

These races go through woods and fields.

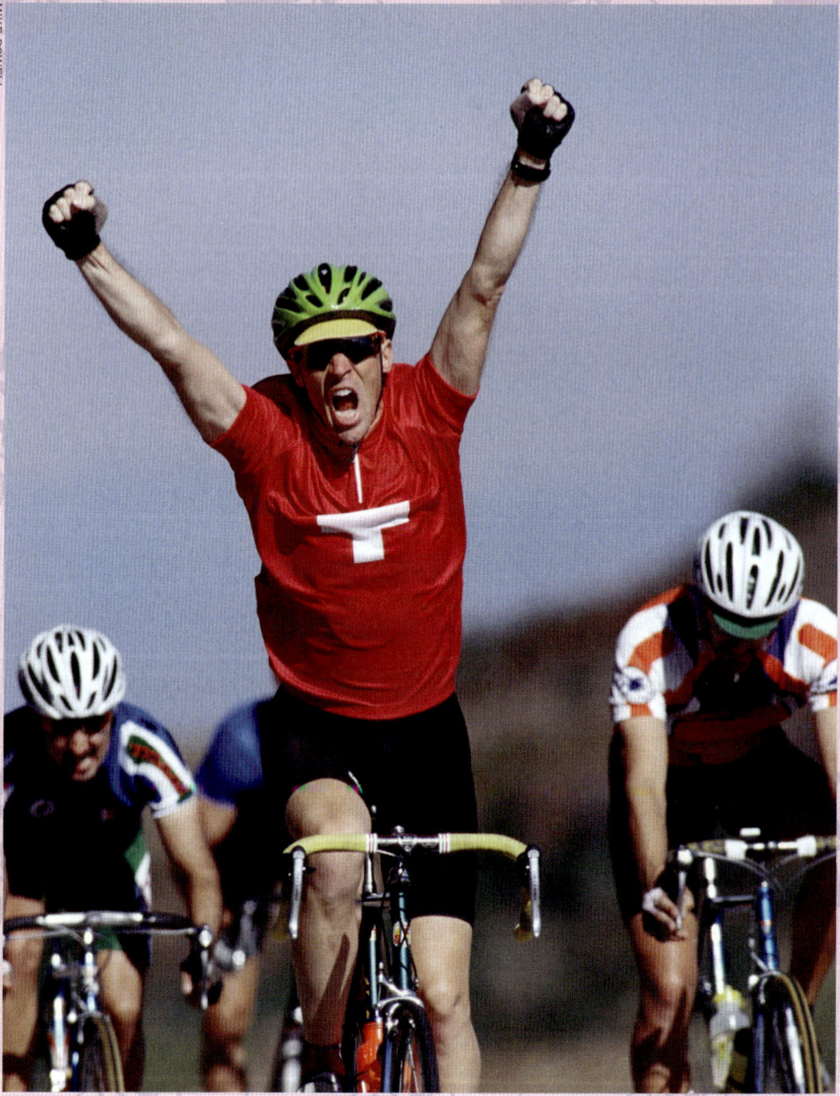

MIKE POWELL

All of the cyclists want to do their best.

In some events, just one person wins a gold medal.

In team races, everyone on the winning team gets a medal.